LON   D0184155   NET

Other books by Allan Ahlberg

A BIT MORE BERT

THE ADVENTURES OF BERT

The FAST FOX, SLOW DOG series (illus. André Amstutz)

FUNNYBONES: THE BLACK CAT (illus. André Amstutz)

FUNNYBONES: BUMPS IN THE NIGHT (illus. André Amstutz)

FUNNYBONES: THE PET SHOP (illus. André Amstutz)

The HAPPY FAMILIES series (illus. various)

THE LITTLE CAT BABY

Other books by Janet and Allan Ahlberg

BURGLAR BILL

BYE BYE BABY

THE CLOTHES HORSE AND OTHER STORIES

COPS AND ROBBERS

EACH PEACH PEAR PLUM

FUNNYBONES

IT WAS A DARK AND STORMY NIGHT

JEREMIAH IN THE DARK WOODS

THE JOLLY CHRISTMAS POSTMAN

THE JOLLY POSTMAN

THE JOLLY POCKET POSTMAN

STARTING SCHOOL

Dinosaur
Dreams

ALLAN AHLBERG • ANDRÉ AMSTUTZ

PUFFIN

In a dark dark street
there is a tall tall house.
In the tall tall house
there is a deep deep cellar.
In the deep deep cellar
there is a cosy cosy bed.
And in the cosy cosy bed . . .

. . . three skeletons are dreaming.
The big skeleton is dreaming
about dinosaurs.
"I knew dinosaurs could run," he says
(in his dream).
"I never knew they had roller skates!"

Suddenly, the big skeleton is chased
by a very big dinosaur.
"You can't scare me," he says.
"You're just a dream."
"Grr!" growls the dinosaur.
"Help!" shouts the big skeleton.
And he runs away.

The little skeleton is dreaming
about dinosaurs too.
"I knew dinosaurs could swim," he says.
"I never knew they had armbands!"

Suddenly, the little skeleton is chased
by a little dinosaur.
"You can't scare me," he says.
"You're just a fossil."
"Grr!" growls the dinosaur.
"Help!" shouts the little skeleton.
And *he* runs away.

The dog skeleton is also dreaming
about dinosaurs.
Suddenly, into his dream
comes the little skeleton
chased by a little dinosaur,
and the big skeleton
chased by a big dinosaur.

The dog skeleton
barks at the dinosaurs:
"Woof!"
And *he* chases *them*!
"Hooray!" says the big skeleton.
"Hooray!" says the little skeleton.
"Give that dog a bone!"

The dinosaurs *hide* away.

But the dog skeleton finds them
and chases them again.
The dinosaurs don't look
where they are going.
Suddenly, there is a great big crash
and a very great big . . .

For some reason
(remember, this is a dream),

the big skeleton
and the little skeleton

put the dinosaur bones
together again.

They make the biggest dinosaur
the world has ever seen . . .

. . . and *it* chases them!

At last the big skeleton
and the little skeleton wake up.
They rub their eyes
and scratch their skulls.
They talk about their dreams.

"I had a dream about dinosaurs,"
says the big skeleton.
"You were in it."
"No, I wasn't," the little skeleton says.
"You were in mine!"

You were in it!

No I wasn't!

After that, the big skeleton says,
"What shall we do now?"
"Let's take the dog for a walk,"
says the little skeleton.
"Good idea!" the big skeleton says.

But the dog skeleton isn't ready for a walk. He is still sleeping. He has a dream bone in his dream mouth . . .

. . . and does not want to be disturbed.

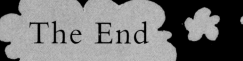

The End